PAM MUÑOZ RYAN

RIDING FREEDOM

DRAWINGS BY

BRIAN SELZNICK

SCHOLASTIC INC.

New York Toronto London Auckland Sydney
Mexico City New Delhi Hong Kong Buenos Aires

BOUQUETS TO
Kendra Marcus, who from the moment
I mentioned Charlotte, said, "Write it."

LAURELS TO
Tracy Mack at Scholastic, who knew
there was a bigger story to tell, and
helped me find it.

GARLANDS TO
The Santa Cruz Historical Society
for their documented research
and direction.

No part of this publication may be reproduced, stored in a retrieval system, or
transmitted in any form or by any means, electronic, mechanical, photocopying,
recording, or otherwise, without written permission of the publisher.
For information regarding permission, write to Scholastic Inc., Attention:
Permissions Department, 557 Broadway, New York, NY 10012.

ISBN-13: 978-0-439-08796-4
ISBN-10: 0-439-08796-1

Text copyright © 1998 by Pam Muñoz Ryan.
Drawings copyright © 1998 by Brian Selznick.
All rights reserved. Published by Scholastic Inc.
SCHOLASTIC and associated logos are trademarks
and/or registered trademarks of Scholastic Inc.

48   15 16 17 18 19 20

Printed in the U.S.A.   40

This edition first printing, June 2007

TO WOMEN OF SUBSTANCE

Sally Dean, Virginia Dowling, Mary Freeman,

Shelley Gill, C. Pamela Green,

and Kathleen Johnson.

In the Beginning

IN THE MID-EIGHTEEN HUNDREDS, when the East was young and the West was yet to be settled, a baby was born, named Charlotte. When she was nothing more than a bundle, she surprised her parents and puzzled the doctor by surviving several fevers. Folks said that any other baby would have died, but Charlotte was already strong. She walked before most babies crawled. She talked before most babies babbled, and she never cried. Unless someone took something away from her.

A few months after Charlotte's second birthday, on a blustery evening, she rode with her parents toward their small farm in the New Hampshire countryside. Their horse-drawn wagon was rickety and swayed back and forth with each gust of wind. Thunder made the horses skittish, and they reared and struggled in their harnesses. Charlotte sat up straight in her mother's lap, watching the trees waving in the wind and listening to the horses' loud whinnies. Her father tried to settle the team, and her mother held Charlotte snugly and sang a song to comfort her. But Charlotte wasn't afraid.

A crack of lightning lit up the countryside and

the horses lurched forward, reeling down the road out of control.

"Hold on!" yelled her father.

"Stop!" screamed her mother. "Keep them straight! Keep them straight!"

Charlotte's mother clutched her closer and tried to hold on as the frantic horses dragged the wagon over the bumpy road.

Her father hollered, "Whoa! Whoa!" but the horses had already lunged down a steep hill crowded with trees and boulders. Tree limbs smacked the horses, frightening them even more. The wagon followed, plunging over the side and smashing into tree trunks before it overturned on a rocky ledge. Charlotte was thrown free of the splintered wagon and landed in a bed of tall grass. Her father and mother were killed instantly.

Unharmed, Charlotte waved to the snuffling horses who were now free of the wagon. Like nursemaids, they hovered around her. At times, they whinnied as if calling for help. Rain drenched the countryside and Charlotte shivered through the night, but the horses stood close by, protecting her from the rain and nuzzling her with their warm breath.

The horses were still keeping watch over Charlotte when neighbors found her the next morning. She was holding so tight to one of the horses' reins that they didn't dare pry it out of her hand.

The old doctor, who had known Charlotte since she was born, wasn't at all surprised that she survived the crash. Instead of taking the horse's rein out of Charlotte's hand, he cut the leather well above her grip.

"She might as well have something to hold on to," he said. "She hasn't got much else. There's no other family to speak of."

The doctor looked up at the people who had found her.

"We got enough mouths to feed," said the man. And he and his wife turned away.

"I hate to think you'll grow up in an orphanage," the doctor said as he carried Charlotte. "But if anybody can make it alone in this world, it's you. Since the day you were born, you've been determined as a mule and tough as a rawhide bone."

1

AFTER TEN YEARS AT THE ORPHANAGE, Charlotte wasn't like most girls her age. And who knew if it was growing up like a follow-along puppy in a pack of ruffian boys, or if it was just her own spit and fire. But she never had a doll or a tea party. She couldn't sew a stitch and she didn't know a petticoat from a pea pod. Wild hairs sprang out of her brown braids, and her ribbons dangled to her waist, untied. Her frock was too big and hung like a sack on her small frame. Smudges of dirt always covered her, and instead of girl-like lace, for as long as anyone could remember, she wore a strip of leather rein tied around her wrist.

Charlotte's greatest misfortune was that Mrs. Boyle, the cook, had been put in charge of her. With the shape and personality of a very large toad, and without a mothering bone in her body, Mrs. Boyle certainly wasn't going to teach Charlotte how to be lady-like. She couldn't be bothered with Charlotte, except to order her around the kitchen. And although Charlotte knew how to boil oats and make mush for an army, and could peel mountains of potatoes and scrub pots and pans, Mrs. Boyle still yelled at her for the littlest things. For being too noisy or too quiet, or for gazing out the window at some horse in the pasture that needed to be ridden. Being in the kitchen was a thorn in Charlotte's side, and she hated it worse than falling in a real briar patch.

Every day Charlotte did her chores in the kitchen as fast as she could. Then she hung up her apron and headed for the only place that made her happy: the stables. Today, Charlotte hurried there with one thing on her mind: winning the pasture race.

As soon as Charlotte approached, the horses started moving toward their gates and hanging their heads over to be petted. The smell of the sweet, dank hay and the horses comforted her like an old quilt on a cold day. The elderly stable master was raking the stalls.

"Hi, Vern. Is Freedom ready for the race?"

"Miss Charlotte, that horse is always ready to run, and as much as she takes a shine to you, I 'spect you could talk her to the moon and back."

Vern was tall and thin, with leathery skin the color of coffee with no milk. He tended the stables with a quiet, gentle nature. He didn't talk much to anyone else, but he loved to tell Charlotte stories, most of them true, that left her in a spell with her mouth wide open.

Vern had named all the horses himself. He always said that naming something was important. That a name ought to stand for something. And that a horse should have a fine name fit for a fine animal. So the horses all had names like Justice and Hope and Charity, and Vern had a story that went with every one of those names. Hope for wanting a better life when he was a young slave on a plantation in Virginia. Charity because of the kindness of the people who had helped him through his struggles. But the story that Charlotte begged for most was the one about Freedom.

Freedom was Charlotte's favorite horse. She had watched her birthing a few years earlier and had babied her ever since. It was on Freedom that Vern taught Charlotte how to ride. She often pestered Vern for the story about Freedom's name. The story of how Vern ran away and hid in a root cellar with nothing but an old shirt to keep him warm. Ran all the way north so he could be free. And named a horse Freedom for something he won.

"You gonna beat William in the race today?" asked Vern.

"I aim to. He deserves to be taken down a peg."

William was thirteen, and he bullied the younger boys. He threw rocks at the cats and kittens, he whipped the horses, and he couldn't stand that Charlotte was better than he was at climbing trees and riding horses.

"I 'spect you will," said Vern. "Freedom trusts you. William's ridin' Justice, and Justice just as soon throw him off. That boy is full of no respect for horses. You know what I always say?"

Charlotte knew it in her heart. "A horse rides the way it's ridden," said Charlotte.

Vern nodded his head, and Charlotte led Freedom from the stall.

The pasture fence was already lined with boys sitting on the top rail, waiting for the races to start. Mr. Millshark, the overseer, walked up and down in front of the starting line waiting for the riders. He was the shortest, fattest, most mean-spirited man that Charlotte had ever known. His beard and hair were almost the same color as his dimpled white skin, and he reminded Charlotte of a plump new potato.

Mr. Millshark was in his glory during pasture races. Instead of his usual scowling self, he paraded around with a smile stuck on his face, clapping people on the back, and shaking hands all around. This was his opportunity to show off and to let people think that the orphanage was a decent place with happy children. But Charlotte and the others knew the truth. The orphanage was nothing more than a work farm, and no matter how young, every child worked hard. Mr. Millshark saw to that.

Charlotte walked toward the pasture, leading Freedom on a halter. The horse nudged her as if to hurry her along.

The boys from town laughed when they saw Charlotte. She ignored them and headed toward the starting line until William and a group of boys blocked her way.

"No girls allowed," said William.

Charlotte tightened her fists and planted her feet. She pursed her lips and glared at William with her piercing blue eyes.

"Get out of my way, William," she said.

Some of the boys stepped back. They had seen that look before.

With disgust he said, "Suit yourself, but you'll be sorry."

The riders mounted and readied the horses. Mr. Millshark raised the flag.

"Go!" he yelled.

The riders hollered at their horses and pressed them to start running.

Charlotte let Freedom start out slow, saving her for a spurt near the finish. William was close behind. Soon the two rode neck-in-neck. But in the second lap, Charlotte let William take the lead. Charlotte knew her horses. Justice was a dobbin, gentle at heart, and didn't take kindly to being ridden hard. William was pressing him, and the poor horse would tire out soon. As they approached the final turn, Charlotte gave Freedom full rein. In a blinding gallop, with her long braids waving behind her like two thick ropes, she passed William and crossed the finish line two lengths ahead.

The townspeople clapped, and Charlotte heard the boys from the orphanage give a wild cheer. She knew why. Most of them had bet money on her to win.

Charlotte slowed Freedom and walked her around the pasture. The horse was breathing heavy and wheezing. She lathered more than usual and felt warm. Too warm.

Vern should take a look at her, thought Charlotte.

As she got near the fence, a man and woman waved at her.

"Hey there!" called the man.

"Hello," said Charlotte.

"You're a good rider," said the woman.

"Thank you, ma'am," said Charlotte.

"So you like horses?"

"Yes, sir, a might more than people."

The man and woman laughed.

Worried about Freedom, Charlotte said, "I have to go now," and she headed toward the barn.

Charlotte patted Freedom's neck. "You okay, girl?"

William caught up to Charlotte.

"You come to congratulate me, William?"

"I hope you like winning 'cause that's the last race you'll ever run."

"And how you gonna stop me, William?"

"I got my ways, and like I said before, you'll be sorry."

"I ain't got time for you, William, I got a sick horse needs tendin'," and Charlotte rode ahead.

But what William said needled her, and when she glanced back, she didn't like what she saw. William was talking to Mr. Millshark. And Mr. Millshark was patting him on the back and listening with a concerned look on his face.

Vern was worried about Freedom.

"The last few days she's been actin' kinda

funny and hasn't been eatin' like usual, but it didn't seem to be nothin' serious. She don't look good now though. Let's put her to bed," he said.

As they rubbed her down, Freedom tried to nip at her own stomach.

"Maybe it's just a touch of colic," Vern reassured Charlotte.

But by the time they got her into the stall, Freedom fell to her knees and then lay down.

"I'm going for some water for the fever," said Vern.

He wouldn't say so, but Charlotte knew it was serious. She knelt next to the horse, stroking her head. Freedom lay motionless, except for her labored breathing. Charlotte swallowed hard to keep back the tears.

"Charlotte! Where are you, Charlotte?"

"Over here, Hay."

Hayward was two years younger, and from the day he'd arrived at the orphanage, he'd latched on to Charlotte. He was persistent and friendly and talked so much that Charlotte often thought he might choke on his words. With hair the color of turnips and ears as big as saucers, he was about the homeliest thing she had ever seen. Although Charlotte sometimes pretended to be annoyed when he pestered her, she didn't really mind. Besides, he needed her.

One afternoon three years ago, soon after Hayward arrived at the orphanage, Charlotte had walked behind the barn to find him taking on William and two other older boys.

"Where did you get those ears! Was your mother an elephant?" yelled William.

"Can you *hear* outta those things, or are they just for decoration?"

"What does your girlfriend, Charlotte, think about them ears?"

Hayward was bloody and bruised but still fighting with a never-give-up-look in his eyes when Charlotte dove in. The three boys were left in worse shape than Hayward. And Hayward and Charlotte had been left with each other.

They had been best friends ever since.

Hayward climbed over the gate into the stall.

"Freedom's real sick," Charlotte said.

Hayward nodded his head. "I'm sorry, Charlotte." And then for once he was quiet.

They lay back in the hay with their arms tucked behind their heads and stared at the light that slivered through the rafters.

"Someday, Hay, we're going to leave this place. You and me and Freedom. I'm going to have a fine ranch and a home. I'll have foals every spring and you can come work for me and train 'em to be fine riding horses."

"Yeah," said Hayward. "And we'll hire a cook. A real good one. And we'll put a sign out front that says PRIVATE PROPERTY so no one as mean as William can ever set foot. Tell again how we're going to get the ranch, Charlotte."

"Well, we'll be here until we're sixteen. First, I'll leave and get a job and save some money. Then, I'll come back for you and we'll go looking for the ranch."

"Let's get a ranch far away from here."

"Don't worry, Hay, it won't be anywhere around here."

Charlotte was silent. She stared at the rafters and listened to the pawing and snorting of the horses in the other stalls. She rolled to her side and stroked Freedom's neck.

"Charlotte, do you remember your parents?"

Hayward liked to tell about his parents. They had died when he was seven so he still remembered them.

Sometimes Charlotte closed her eyes and tried to bring back a memory. Any memory. She could almost see a face. But since she'd never seen any portraits of her parents, she only imagined what they looked like. All she really remembered was being held tightly in someone's lap, and images of horses.

"No, Hay, I don't remember. Tell me about yours again."

But before he could answer, they heard the old porch bell ring one clang. There was a pause. Then it rang two clangs. Another pause. Then three clangs.

Charlotte and Hayward sat up and stared at each other.

That was the signal for all the boys to line up by the front steps. It meant that one of the families that visited the orphanage today wanted a closer look at one of the boys.

It meant someone would be adopted.

2

CHARLOTTE WATCHED FROM THE stable as Mr. Millshark walked up and down in front of the line of boys, beaming. The prospective parents followed him. Now and then they stopped to say a few words to one of the boys, but usually just to the younger ones.

Charlotte had stopped lining up a long time ago. She was never considered for adoption anyway. People wanted boys to help with their farms, or a son to carry on the family name, or they wanted someone young and cute.

Once, when Charlotte had been as-cute-as-they-come, a couple came through the kitchen with Mr. Millshark. The wife saw Charlotte standing on a stool, washing dishes.

"Oh! I had been hoping for a girl, but they said there were only boys here," said the woman. She smiled at Charlotte with warm, come-home-with-me eyes.

With as much politeness as Charlotte could muster, she said, "Yes, ma'am, it's boys, 'cept me," and she smiled back at the woman.

The woman walked over to her and took her soapy little hand. For an instant, Charlotte hoped beyond hope.

But Mrs. Boyle marched over and scooped Charlotte into her arms.

"This here's my niece just helpin' out in the kitchen. She ain't for adoptin'. C'mon, Charlotte."

Before Charlotte could say a word, Mrs. Boyle carried her out the backdoor and took her to the garden to pick beans.

After that, Mrs. Boyle hid her in the potato bin each time people came through, for fear of losing her kitchen maid. Charlotte remembered the dark, crowded bin and lying on the lumpy potatoes. She would hear Mr. Millshark saying,

"And this is the kitchen where Mrs. Boyle prepares our meals."

She remembered peering through the cracks in the wooden slats at the people who came through. Sometimes Charlotte wanted to push open the lid and jump out and yell, "I'm here! I would like a home! Me! Take me!" But more often than not, Mrs. Boyle sat on top of the bin so Charlotte couldn't budge, and Charlotte knew better than to make a peep until the people had gone.

Charlotte went back to the horses. What would be the point of lining up with the boys anyway? Even though Mrs. Boyle couldn't hide her in the potato bin anymore, nobody wanted an almost-grown girl.

Freedom seemed worse. Vern hovered around her for an hour trying to figure out what was wrong. He just kept shaking his head, and Charlotte got a bad feeling deep inside.

Later, as Charlotte served the soup at dinner, Hayward whispered, "We heard someone got adopted. Maybe it'll be William."

"Nah," said Charlotte. "We ain't that lucky."

"Who do you think, Charlotte?" asked Hay.

But Charlotte didn't answer. Any other time she would be as nosy as the rest about who it was, but all she could think about was Freedom.

As soon as she finished the dishes, she went back to the stable. She wanted to do something, anything, to make Freedom better. She sat next to the filly until well after midnight when Vern finally sent her to bed.

"We won't know nothin' till the morning," he said.

Reluctantly, Charlotte returned to her room. She tossed all night anxious for morning, but she knew she couldn't check on the horse until after breakfast. Would she survive? Sweet Freedom. She just had to make it.

Charlotte tried to hurry through the Sunday morning dishes but Mrs. Boyle would have none of that.

"Charlotte, don't you be givin' those dishes a lick and a promise. You scrub those pans until they're clean!" she yelled.

Charlotte thought she'd never finish. When she finally bolted out the kitchen door,

Hayward was waiting at the back steps.

"Let's go check on Freedom," said Charlotte, almost running.

"Charlotte, wait! I heard who's been adopted," said Hayward as he hurried to keep up.

"Yeah? Was it one of the young'uns?"

"No," said Hayward. He stopped right where he was and waited for Charlotte to turn around and look at him.

"Well, if it ain't William I don't really care," said Charlotte. "I don't care much about anything right now except Freedom. You coming or not?"

Hayward hesitated. "Yeah, I'm coming," he said.

They hurried to the barn. Freedom's stall was empty.

"Vern must have moved her to the small corral to let her get some air," said Charlotte.

They turned and started toward the pasture. But when Charlotte saw Vern walking toward her, his face told it all.

"The infection got the best of her, Miss Charlotte."

"No!" Charlotte clenched her hands.

"Me and some of the older boys buried her behind the south pasture. Been out there all mornin'. She went real easy in her sleep. There was nothing we could do."

Charlotte nodded. She squeezed her eyes tight.

"She was a real nice horse," said Vern.

"Yeah," said Charlotte, but she didn't cry. She never cried.

"Ain't no shame in mournin' a loss, Miss Charlotte," he said.

But Charlotte pretended she hadn't heard him and walked over to a stall and called to the stallion. He came over and nuzzled Charlotte's hand.

"You sure have a way with them horses," said Vern.

Charlotte nodded as she stroked the horse's head.

"You go right ahead and rake them stalls if you a mind to it. You the best stable boy I got," said Vern. "Sometimes I don't know what I'd do without you in here tendin' to these animals. You my right hand in this stable, Miss Charlotte."

Charlotte forced a smile.

A feeling crept up into her throat and made it hard to swallow. She felt like she was on the verge of something. She tried to shake it off. When she couldn't, she grabbed a rake and started working.

She tried to concentrate on the raking, but all she could see was her last glimpse of Freedom, lying in the straw, breathing heavy, her eyes closed.

"Charlotte?" said Hayward.

She had forgotten about Hayward. He had wanted to tell her something.

But before she could ask, Mr. Millshark's stern voice startled her.

"Charlotte!" he yelled. Charlotte couldn't remember Mr. Millshark ever setting foot in the stables. Vern stood up immediately, and Hayward, who was even scared of Millshark's shadow, fled to the tack room to hide.

"Vern, just a few words with Charlotte and I'll be on my way," said Mr. Millshark as he turned to Charlotte.

"It's been brought to my attention that some of the townspeople don't think it's quite lady-like for you to be racing the boys. Our reputation here is of raising strong, strapping young men, and we can't have folks calling our boys mollycoddles now, can we? You're getting close to being a young lady and you need to start acting like one. From now on, you will have full duties in the kitchen with Mrs. Boyle. The stable is off limits to you."

Vern looked up from his work. He never questioned Mr. Millshark, but he said, "She's a help in the stables. She does the work of three of them boys and she knows the horses as good as me."

"Is that so?" said Mr. Millshark. "I heard that she rode a sick horse in the race yesterday and that the horse died this morning. A young man wouldn't have made such a foolish decision. She'll stay in the kitchen where she belongs."

Mr. Millshark turned and left.

Charlotte looked at Vern.

"He's got a cold heart, Miss Charlotte. And you know you had nothin' to do with Freedom dyin'. I'm real, real sorry. Maybe he'll change his notion."

Charlotte couldn't speak.

She ran from the stables. She ran hard,

without stopping, toward the tree line behind the pasture. She hated this place. Mr. Millshark would never, ever change his mind.

Hayward called after her. "Charlotte, wait!"

She slumped against a tree and bent over to catch her breath.

Hayward caught up to her.

"Charlotte, you all right?"

"I don't know, Hay. Stinkin' old Millshark! I can't think of nothin' worse than not workin' with the horses. I can't wait to leave this place. Whoever got adopted is lucky not to have to look at Millshark's face ever again."

"I've been trying to tell you, Charlotte . . ."

Hayward looked down at the ground and drew a circle in the dirt with his boot. He didn't say anything. Just kept looking at the dirt.

"Hayward, what's got into you?"

"It ain't William who got adopted. Well, you see . . . . uh . . . it was me. It's a family from Nashua. Name is Clark. Their boy died so they came here to get one to take his place and that's me. I met 'em this morning, and the lady kept patting me on the head and the man kept calling me son. I guess they don't mind about my ears."

Charlotte stared at Hayward like he was talking crazy talk. Surely it couldn't really be true. Why, Hayward was ten. He couldn't leave now. They had plans. She took a deep breath and felt her stomach do a flip-flop.

A voice came out of her mouth, but it sounded strange and shaky. "That's real nice, Hay."

"I asked them if they wanted a girl, too, but I guess they don't."

Charlotte looked out over the pasture and nodded her head as if Hay were telling her some everyday news.

"Uh . . . well then . . . when you leaving?" she asked.

"Tomorrow morning."

Charlotte nodded again. Tomorrow was Monday. They always helped Vern soap the bridles on Monday.

" 'Course they could still change their minds. Do you think they'll change their minds, Charlotte?"

Charlotte looked at his worried face. Getting adopted was what every boy lived for. Even Charlotte had those dreams. Dreams of a home. Dreams of a family. At least Hayward would be in a better place than the orphanage. She shook her head and reassured him.

"Nah." She reached out and ruffled his hair. "You're just what they want, kid."

Charlotte sat down under the maple. She felt like someone had socked the wind from her. Her hands shook. She sat on them to keep them still. Hayward sat down next to her.

"I'll write you, Charlotte. Then you'll be the only one here that gets letters."

She looked at Hayward. His ears stuck out hard from under his cap. Charlotte closed her eyes. She realized that she had been hoping for something for a long time. She'd been hoping Hayward's ears would keep him at the orphanage forever.

"Charlotte?"

She opened her eyes and said calmly, "I'm leaving, too."

Hayward looked at her like she'd lost her mind. "You can't. You're not old enough. The last boy that run off got caught and owed the overseer two more years past sixteen."

Charlotte felt a determined anger welling up inside her.

"Hayward, don't try to talk sense into me. You're leavin' tomorrow. I can't work with the horses. You know that Mr. Millshark will think of some reason to keep me here forever. I ain't workin' in that kitchen for the rest of my days! You and me got plans."

Hayward jumped up. "They'll find you, Charlotte. They always find the runaways. And Millshark, he's mean. He'll punish you!"

"He can't if he doesn't catch me," said Charlotte. "I just know I ain't stayin' here to deal with William and Millshark and ol' Mrs. Boyle. Not without you or Freedom or the horses to keep me company. Now I got to think of a way!"

Charlotte knew that a young girl couldn't travel without a chaperon. She stood up and put her hands on her hips and paced around in a circle, staring at the ground. She kicked at a rock until it flew into the air and landed in the pasture. She would need money to leave. And when she got away, where would she go? She would need a job. Who would hire her?

"Don't do it, Charlotte."

Charlotte looked at him. She looked at his

hair stuffed under his cap, his overalls hanging crooked to one side. She already missed him, and he hadn't even gone yet. It wasn't fair. None of it was fair. Not even that she couldn't travel alone. A young boy like Hayward could travel around without question.

As she considered this, a tendril of an idea began to weave itself around in her mind.

And a plan began to take shape.

"I got to, Hay," she said. "But I'm going to need your help."

3

"CHARLOTTE, YOU LOOK NERVOUS AS A cat," said Hayward.

Charlotte looked around to see if anyone was watching. She took the bundle he was holding and stuffed it in the wood box behind the kitchen.

"It's all there, Charlotte. Everything you asked for. The overalls, the cap, the boots . . . everything. Please be careful, Charlotte."

"Thanks, Hay. I don't know what I'da done without you."

Hayward was ready to leave. His new family was waiting around front. Charlotte tried to look at him but she couldn't. She looked at the ground.

"Charlotte, how will I know where to find you?"

"I know where you'll be," she said. "I'll find you again, I promise. Anyway, I've got something for you to remember me."

Charlotte took a narrow piece of leather out of her apron pocket.

"But that's your bracelet," said Hayward.

"No, I cut it in two, long ways. See?"

Charlotte held up her wrist. The leather that she had worn since she was a baby was half as wide. She tied the other half around Hayward's wrist. He was quiet and his eyes were wet. He put his arms around her and buried his head against her apron.

Charlotte held him and ruffled his hair. She felt sick inside, like she'd swallowed something spoiled.

"Now get along. They'll be looking for you."

Hayward straightened up. Muddy streaks ran down his face.

"Good-bye, Charlotte," he said, walking backward, still looking at her.

"Good-bye, Hay. I'll find you. We're gonna have a ranch, remember? With a big ol' sign that says PRIVATE PROPERTY. Remember? And foals every spring . . ."

She couldn't finish. She choked on the tears as they spilled down her cheeks. She tried to stop but she couldn't. They just flowed a river down her face until she couldn't see him anymore.

Charlotte sat behind the wood box for nearly an hour. She felt achy and empty. Silent, her tears spent, she looked out over the pastures and wondered where she'd be tomorrow. It would be easy to stay here and just go about her business. At least she'd know where she'd be sleeping every night. She'd have regular meals. But she wouldn't have the things she loved. What did Vern always say? That the easy way ain't always going to get you anywhere.

Mrs. Boyle's voice startled her. "Charlotte, do I have to come out there and get the wood myself? You're good for nothin' and slow as molasses!"

Charlotte jumped up and gathered the wood and carried it into the kitchen. She didn't want Mrs. Boyle getting her dander up and poking her nose in the wood box. Not today.

When Charlotte walked back into the kitchen and saw the piles of potatoes waiting for her, she realized that as nervous as she was about running away, she was more afraid to stay. Something bigger than peeling potatoes was nagging at her on the inside. But she still needed help to make her plan work. And there was only one person left who she considered her friend.

Vern always ate dinner in the kitchen, so afterward, when he came out to the kitchen steps, Charlotte was waiting.

"Well, Miss Charlotte! I already been missin' you, and those horses already missin' you, too."

Charlotte put her finger up to her lips and waved Vern away from the back steps. When they were safely out of Mrs. Boyle's earshot, Charlotte looked at him and gathered her courage.

"Vern, where would somebody pick up a stage around here?"

"A stage? Well, the southbound picks up in Concord ev'ry Tuesday and Saturday morning, so there's one comin' tomorrow. You remember Concord. You rode over there with me to pick up some feed. That's 'bout all I know. Why? What are you up to?"

"How much does it cost?" asked Charlotte.

Vern studied her.

"Well, it costs some dollars to get a body to the next stop. But that ain't very far. You got money for a stage ride, Miss Charlotte?"

"Vern, you know I ain't got no money. But, I . . . I got to leave. I ain't got no good cause to stay here. The only reason they keep me is to take Mrs. Boyle's place in the kitchen."

Worried furrows crinkled up Vern's forehead.

"Runnin' away is a might dangerous thing to do," said Vern.

"You ran away once," said Charlotte.

Vern tilted his hat back on his head and looked at her.

"Yes, I did. I never knew my momma or poppa, just like you. I ran from the South to the North and all I left behind was bein' somebody's slave. But when I ran, I had folks that helped me. And hid me. You're a girl. That's different," said Vern.

"It ain't that different," said Charlotte.

Vern looked at her, then toward the kitchen.

"Well, maybe you're right. If anybody would wither and die in a kitchen, it's you," he said.

She straightened her shoulders and looked at him directly.

"I'm goin', Vern."

He shook his head then lowered his voice to a whisper. "Miss Charlotte, anybody know your intentions?"

"No."

"Almighty, you keep it that way." Vern looked around to see if anyone could hear. "Now, you gotta make it look like lots of things could've happened to you so folks won't know which way you went. And . . . you need to look different."

"I already got that figured out."

"I just bet you do," said Vern.

"I . . . I need . . . a pair of scissors tonight," said Charlotte. "And some money for the stage. I could pay you back . . . not right off but down the line."

"I don't know what you have in mind, Miss Charlotte, and it's better I don't, 'cause Mr.

Millshark, he'll be askin' me 'bout you first thing. I'll try my best to getcha those things. You be careful. You hear me? You be real careful. You're headin' for Concord, right? So let me think. You know I can't read a scratch so when you get through the woods and come to the town sign, you pile some rocks up around the base of that sign. That way, next week when I get the feed and I see those rocks, I'll know you made it that far. I'll be worried sick till then."

Charlotte smiled at Vern. She would've hugged him, too, if she hadn't been worried about Mrs. Boyle walking out of the kitchen any minute. She couldn't let anyone think that Vern might have helped her.

"Thanks, Vern. I wish I could stay with you and work with the horses, but . . . I'd be in the kitchen and I'd be missin' Justice and frettin' 'cause I wouldn't get to see Charity's foal . . . or help you name it."

"I know. I know, Miss Charlotte," said Vern. "You gotta do what your heart tells you."

"I won't ever forget you," said Charlotte.

"I guess I'm not likely to forget you, Miss Charlotte. And don't you worry 'bout Charity's foal. I got me a name all picked out for that one, and you did help me. Just came to me. A fine name that stands up real good. Fittin' for the fine horse it will be. That foal's gonna be named Charlotte's Pride."

Charlotte lay in bed, in her clothes, until after midnight. She thought about Hayward, sleeping in his very own bed, in his very own house with his new family. She wondered what that felt like. Knowing you were home. Knowing there were people in the very next room who cared about you.

"Don't forget me, Hay," she whispered into her pillow.

When Charlotte was certain that everyone was asleep, she got up and plumped her pillows and laid them in her bed, covering them with the blankets so it looked like she was still sleeping. She crawled out the window and sneaked to the wood box.

Although the night was clear and bright with moonlight, the wood box was in shadows. Had Vern come through? Charlotte opened the box. Inside was Hayward's bundle of clothes. She strained her eyes in the dim light. And there, in the corner, was another smaller cloth bundle tied with string. She looked back toward the barn. Thank you, Vern, she thought.

She grabbed the two bundles and ran as fast as she could until she was beyond the far pasture. The road to Concord was on the other side of the woods and she would have to hurry to get there by morning.

In the safety of the trees, she unwrapped Vern's bundle. He had put the money in a little leather pouch. And there was a sandwich and the shears that they used to trim the horses' manes. But more than that, the cloth they were wrapped in was a worn piece of a shirt that had been crudely hemmed the size of a large kerchief. One side of the kerchief still had the original buttonholes. Charlotte rubbed it over her cheek. She could still hear Vern saying, "You gotta do what your heart tells you."

She found a pool near a fast-moving stream. Then she untied her ribbons, unbraided her hair, and shook it hard. It surrounded her shoulders like a woman's shawl. She leaned over and looked at herself in the water.

"Good-bye, Charlotte," she whispered.

With a trembling hand, she picked up the scissors and cut off a hank of hair. With every snip, long locks landed in the water and floated downstream in the strong current. She had never cared all that much about her hair, but now she ached for it as it disappeared. She dropped her hair ribbons into the water, and like silky snakes, they drifted away, too.

When Charlotte stood up, she was surprised at how light-headed she felt, as if those braids had been holding her fast to the ground. She quickly changed into Hay's clothes and put the sandwich and the money pouch in the big pocket of the overalls. She folded Vern's makeshift kerchief and tucked it into another smaller pocket.

She took one last look in the pool. The water reflected the image of a young boy.

Quickly, Charlotte stuffed her frock and the scissors in the stump of a dead tree, covering them with damp leaves and brush. She floated her apron in the stream, wrapping the strings around the nearby tree brambles so it wouldn't drift away. *Make it look like different things could have*

happened. If anyone came looking, they'd see her apron and think she had drowned.

Charlotte cut through the woods and arrived at the main road to Concord with the moon still high. She ran until she got tired, then walked, then ran some more. The stage came early, she reminded herself. But her side had a stitch from running, and she slowed a little. Mrs. Boyle would be fussing when Charlotte didn't show up for breakfast chores on time, but she'd be too busy to come looking herself. Eventually, she'd send one of the boys. He'd see the bed, with what looked like Charlotte inside, and try to wake her. The boy would report back that Charlotte was missing and then Mrs. Boyle would be furious. She'd march straight to Mr. Millshark.

Charlotte held her side and started running again. She couldn't miss that stage.

4

BEFORE DAWN, CHARLOTTE CAME UPON the wooden sign for Concord. She stopped and gathered some rocks and piled them up around the base. She pictured Vern riding into town next week and seeing her signal, nodding his head and smiling to himself. At least, she hoped it would be that way. She still had to get on the stage without getting caught.

Charlotte sat on the bench in front of the livery office and ate the sandwich Vern had packed. A sign in the window said SOUTHBOUND COACH 6:00 A.M. Charlotte figured that with luck Mrs. Boyle wouldn't know for sure that she was gone until about 7:00. By that time, she just had to be far enough away. When the ticket office opened, she gathered Vern's coins and bought a one-way to Manchester.

Charlotte's heart leaped when she heard the pounding hooves. She looked toward the end of the road where it led into town. Then, out of a dust cloud, she saw the horses.

Harnessed, six handsome, great-limbed horses trotted toward her. They were mostly gray mustangs, but there was one bay. And a sorrel, like Freedom. Healthy and well tended, they seemed eager to work in the traces that wove them together. Behind them, the driver sat atop the stagecoach, holding the reins, in perfect control. Charlotte had heard about six and eight horses being hitched at one time, but she'd never seen it. What would it feel like to have that many horses step to your call?

The driver yelled, "Whoa!" and the horses slowed.

There was a jingling and rattling and creaking when the coach settled in front of the hotel. The pressure brake screeched as the driver secured the wheels.

The coach gleamed with varnish in the

morning sun. The wheels were painted yellow, and printed on the doors were the words U.S. MAIL. It was the most beautiful thing that Charlotte had ever seen. She walked over and rubbed her hand across the shiny hickory wood. Then she petted the horse that reminded her, too much, of Freedom.

The driver assigned the seats right away. Charlotte climbed aboard and found herself wedged between two plump women.

"Hello there, young man," said one of the women.

Charlotte nodded.

"I'm Mrs. Mapes and this is Mrs. Earhart, my traveling companion. What's your name?"

Charlotte stared blankly at Mrs. Mapes.

"My name?" she asked.

"Yes, your name, dear?"

"Charley," said Charlotte. "My name's Charley."

"Well, Charley, it's nice to meet you. We're traveling to the end of the line so I guess we're in for a long ride together."

"Yes, ma'am," said Charlotte, and pulled the cap tighter over her head.

The stage began rolling and rocking over the countryside. Charlotte watched farms and lush woods moving across the coach window. She wished she could sit up-top with the driver so she could see more. Watch him drive the team. Ask him about the horses' names. She felt excited, as if something new and good was about to happen. What was Hayward doing today, waking up in his new home? She would have a home someday. But not if she'd stayed at the orphanage. Millshark and Mrs. Boyle would've seen to that. Now, she felt certain that anything was possible. Vern used to say that plants can't breathe and grow in a box that's too tight. Now she knew what he meant.

Soon Charlotte fell sound asleep against Mrs. Mapes. She woke up now and then, but with the two ladies droning on with their gossip, and the rocking of the stagecoach, she quickly slipped back into her slumber, happy to be traveling farther and farther away from the orphanage.

It was hours later when the stage pulled in to the end of the line in Worcester, Massachusetts. Why hadn't someone woken Charlotte up and

made her get off sooner? She didn't recognize the driver. Drivers must have changed at one of the stops. Maybe he thought she was with the two women. She *had* fallen asleep against one of them.

After the new driver helped the passengers out of the cramped coach, Charlotte stretched and stood in the street looking up one side and down the other. Guests headed toward the hotel with their satchels and luggage. A burst of laughter erupted from the pub. People came and went from the shops on the street, some in fancier clothes than Charlotte had ever seen. The other passengers drifted away to their destinations and Charlotte soon found herself alone on the side of the road.

What should she do with herself? She'd run away but she had nowhere to go, really. She didn't know a soul. She had no money except for a few remaining coins. She hadn't thought this far. It was getting dark and suddenly she felt frightened and lonely.

Charlotte went over and stroked the horses. At least they felt familiar. The driver came around and started leading the team toward the livery.

"Want some help?" asked Charlotte.

The driver began unhitching the team. "No thankee. I take care of my horses myself. But you're welcome to watch me put 'em to bed." The driver chuckled. "Boys and horses. Can't seem to keep 'em apart."

Charlotte followed him into the stable and watched him take the harnesses off the horses, rub the horses down, and put them in their stalls.

"I can cart some water for you," said Charlotte.

"Good boy, do it then."

Charlotte hauled buckets of water to the stalls, talking to the horses as she went. Then she helped the driver fork in the straw.

"You're right handy with them chores," he said.

"Yes, sir," said Charlotte.

"You live around here?"

"No, sir, well, I just moved to these parts."

"Well, get along now. I'll be closing the barn."

Charlotte backed away and moved toward the main door, stopping and petting each horse as she went. It was safe here. She looked around and noticed the lofts above her. When the driver disappeared into the tack room to hang up some bridles, Charlotte took a chance.

As fast as she could, she climbed up a ladder and flung herself into the loft. She kept her head down and lay there without moving or making a sound. Her heart was pounding as loud as a drum beating. Could the driver hear it, too? He was below her now, whistling and finishing his chores. Finally, he walked out and shut the big barn doors for the night.

Charlotte peeked over the loft into the stalls. Vern would be fussing a blue streak if he saw how poorly these stalls were kept. She wasn't that tired, but she was hungry. She climbed down and started nosing around the barn. There wasn't a bite of food anywhere. Out of habit, she picked up a rake and started cleaning a stall. Then she straightened the bridles in the tack room. Later, she climbed back into the loft. Her stomach growled and complained but finally, she slept.

She dreamed about mush and potatoes and soup.

The next morning, Charlotte woke to the sounds of a busy stable. Stock tenders called to one another. Bridles and traces jangled. The stable master barked out orders.

Charlotte peered over the edge of the loft and barely moved. She couldn't just climb down and appear. They might throw her out. She listened to the comings-and-goings for some hours until things settled down. Maybe it was lunchtime.

When no one was moving about and all she could hear was the blow and whinnies of the horses, she pushed up the loft window. It opened onto a low roof. She quietly climbed out, shinnied down a wooden support beam, and landed behind the main barn.

Hungrier than she could ever remember, she went to the general store and with her remaining money bought some apples. She kept hidden, mainly behind buildings, moving from place to place every hour or so. Before dark, she watched some boys having races in a field. It would have been easy to join them. Easy to beat them all. But there were too many questions that Charlotte didn't want to answer. Besides, if Millshark were looking for her, everyone would know about a new kid who could run circles around the rest.

After the boys got called home for supper, she stayed hidden until dark settled in. She thought about the home-cooked meals they'd be eating. Several times, she took out the kerchief that Vern had made for her and fingered the button-holes. She wondered at all the places it had been. And all the places it was going.

When there was no more activity at the stables, she climbed back in the loft window and quietly waited until the barn was closed for the night. Again, she cleaned the stalls. She wondered how long she could keep doing this. And again she had trouble sleeping, fitfully tossing in the hayloft with dreams of running and running and almost being caught.

When she woke, someone was standing over her with a pitchfork aimed at her face.

5

CHARLOTTE STOOD UP AND BACKED
away from the solid-looking, bald-pated man.

"What're you doing in my stable?" he said.

"I-I needed a place to sleep. I'm sorry," said
Charlotte.

"You the one who cleaned my stalls?"

"Yes, sir."

He lowered the pitchfork and looked at
Charlotte closely.

She reached down and grabbed her cap and
pulled it on.

"You're a scrawny-lookin' thing," said the
man.

"Yes, sir."

"You live around here?"

"Uh, I just moved to these parts. I'm-I'm looking for a job."

"Where're your folks?" he asked.

"They . . . they live out past town. We're on hard times so . . . so they sent me in to find work."

"How'd you get in here?"

"I helped the stage driver bed his horses . . ."

"Well, I don't need any help. You need to get on home."

Charlotte wanted to say that she didn't have a home. She wanted to say that she was on her own and that she needed help. But she knew she couldn't say those things. She didn't know this man. He might turn her in to Millshark, for all she knew.

"I'll . . . I'll work for free if I can sleep and eat here. I can soap those bridles for you. Make 'em look like new."

The man rubbed his hand over his bald head.

"I'm the best groomer around. I can ride and I can . . ."

His face softened. "Well, you did a right smart job on the stalls. The bridles are pretty pitiful. I could use a bit of help. But I'm moving my stables to Rhode Island in a few months. Providence. So don't be getting ideas about staying long. You can sleep in the loft, since you're already doing it. I've been mucking and raking for weeks without a boy. But I don't tolerate no trouble."

"No, sir," said Charlotte.

"Name's Ebeneezer Balch. Go on over and eat at the cafe. Tell 'em I sent you. Then come back and get to work. You sure are scrawny for a growin' boy!"

Ebeneezer told her that he'd gone through more stable boys than he cared to count and that they all had been as lazy as pigs. Charlotte was determined to show him that she was reliable. She put in long hours in the busy stable, cleaning stalls, forking hay, and grooming and feeding the horses. She was the first one up in the morning and the last in bed at night. If there was time, she mended harnesses without being asked. She kept thinking that, just maybe, if she worked hard enough, Ebeneezer would need help in Rhode Island.

But more than that, she loved the horses,

always talking and clucking to them like they were her babies. Before long she could coax even the stubborn ones to do almost anything, with just the murmurings of her voice. The stock tenders shook their heads in amazement. And more than once, Charlotte caught Ebeneezer watching her with the horses.

She'd been there several months when he came into the tack room. He looked unhappy.

"Charley, sit down."

Charlotte knew what was coming. All the preparations had been made to move the business. An uncertain fear crept over her. What would she do after Ebeneezer left?

Ebeneezer cleared his throat and said, "A man was in town this morning tellin' about a runaway girl from an orphanage all the way over in New Hampshire. Said she might have drowned in the river, but might have lived, too. He's going up and down the stage line looking for her. Wanted to know if I knew anything about her 'cause, hear tell, she's real good with horses. She come up missing about the time you showed up here. You know anything about her?"

Charlotte looked down at the bridle she held

in her hands. She felt the blood draining from her face.

"No, sir," she said. She didn't like lying to Ebeneezer.

"Well, I told him I never seen or heard nothin'. He wanted to know if I had a stable boy. I didn't like the looks or the sounds of him one bit. Said he was ready to punish the girl and wanted to find her in the worst way. Hmmph! Acted like he wanted to come pokin' around my stables. I told him there ain't no use, that all I had around my place was top-notch stock tenders. Ain't that right?"

"Yes, sir," said Charlotte.

"Anyhow, ain't been no girls around here, has there?"

Ebeneezer stepped back and looked at Charlotte in a way that he never had before. Did he know?

Charlotte winced. "No, sir," she said.

"Well, that's what I told him. So, she probably *did* drown. Yep, that's what I think. Drowned in the river. Ain't that sad."

He cleared his throat again.

"Now, another thing. I don't think this

fellow's going to give up easy, cocky as he is. I suspect he'll be askin' around town and probably showin' up here to ask questions. Everyone knows I got a new hand."

Charlotte nodded. Her mouth felt dry. What if Millshark showed up here and Ebeneezer got in trouble for hiring her?

The thought of Mr. Millshark finding her and taking her back to the orphanage made her palms sweaty. Made her heart pound. Maybe she should leave. But leaving would mean she'd have to start all over again. She would need to find someplace else to work. And sleep. And eat.

And hide.

Charlotte stood up and dropped the bridle. She edged toward the door.

"I-I need to get on home, you know, since you're moving the stables and all. I best get going."

Ebeneezer held up both of his hands to block her way.

"Just stay put," he said. "Now listen. In all my days, I only seen one other person could work with the horses like you. Could put a spell on them and could ride . . . could ride like . . .

well, I only seen it one other time. I got me a notion and maybe I'm crazy but I got to see if I'm
right. If you can do what I think you can do, I'm
not about to let you go."

As Ebeneezer walked out of the tack room,
he said, "Bring around six. I need a wagon
hitched."

Charlotte tried to concentrate on what he'd
said. Bring around six horses? Do what he
thought she could do? Confused, she found the
traces for six-in-the-hand and brought the horses
around, one at a time, to hitch them.

When each horse was secured to the traces,
Ebeneezer said, "Charley, you drive."

Charlotte stared at Ebeneezer.

"I . . . I ain't drove six-in-the-hand before,"
she said. "I drove two, but not six."

"I know that," said Ebeneezer. "Get up here
and let's take a run, unless you're scared?"

"I ain't scared," said Charlotte.

She climbed into the wagon. What was
Ebeneezer up to? She felt like he was testing
her, almost daring her to drive the team. He
handed her the whip, but she wouldn't take it.

She'd never whipped a horse in her life.

"It's for guiding your team by the sound. Not for beating on a poor horse. Now, here are the ribbons, same as the reins. Hold 'em in your left hand and keep the whip in your right," he said.

She took the whip and the ribbons and listened.

"Each of these pairs of ribbons controls two horses so when you're driving six, you're holding three pairs of ribbons. It ain't as easy as it looks. Here's the pressure brake on the right. Use your foot to work it. Now, release the brake and take her out a mile and turn around."

Since the day Charlotte had caught the stage in Concord, she'd wanted to try a six-horse team. Wanted to know what it felt like behind all those horses. Suddenly, she was getting her chance.

She yelled, "Git along!"

Charlotte held the ribbons lightly and tried to keep the wagon straight on the road, but it veered to the right and then to the left. She had hitched enough teams to understand how the reins worked but Ebeneezer was right, it wasn't as easy as it looked. No one had to tell her though, not to whip the horses.

Charlotte gave gentle tugs on the ribbons but even a slight pull sent the horses in another direction. As she approached the turn, the reins tangled. Some horses turned and some didn't. The wagon rolled into the horses and suddenly she was in the middle of a heap of harnesses and horses. Ebeneezer climbed out and set everything right.

"Guess I was wrong," he said and gave her a peculiar look. "Maybe you're just too young to learn the ribbons. Let's head back."

"I ain't ready to turn back," Charlotte said, and she began to feel that her escape from Mr. Millshark depended on being able to drive this team.

Ebeneezer climbed back in and Charlotte set out. With a steadier hand, she pulled the horses back on course. She tried another turn and again, muddled the horses and wagon. Ebeneezer got out and straightened the lines.

Before he could say anything, Charlotte reached for the reins.

"I can do it," she insisted.

Charlotte took the reins again and again. Although she continued to get jumbled up in the

turns, with each run she felt an exhilaration that she had never felt before. Here were six strong horses waiting for her commands, her tugs on the reins, to tell them which way to go. She yelled, "Haw" and "Gee" to get them to bear left and right, like she did when she was riding one horse or driving two.

She wished Hayward could see her. And Vern. Vern would have never let her get out of that wagon until she figured out the turns. Just like when he taught her to ride, he kept putting her back on Freedom after each fall, saying, "Every time you fall, you learn somethin' new 'bout your horse. You learn what not to do next time."

That's what was happening with the team. Every time she mixed up the reins, she knew what she had done wrong, and she tried not to do it again.

After a dozen runs, she brought them around clean. Ebeneezer finally nodded his approval with a small satisfied smile. He had wanted her to figure it out. He had wanted her to be able to drive the team. But why?

When they pulled back up to the stables, Ebeneezer said, "Charley, or whoever you are, I need this team and this wagon driven to my new stables and I'm figurin' you can drive them. But you need to leave in the morning, before first light. And there's something else, I don't need more stable boys in Rhode Island, but I need another stock tender and soon I'll be needin' coach drivers. You got a lot to learn, but I could train you, if it suits you."

She couldn't stop the grin that spread over her face.

"It suits me fine," she said.

In the Middle

AFTER YEARS OF DRIVING HUNDREDS
of practice runs with Ebeneezer, Charlotte
knew how to coddle a coach around any precari-
ous turn. When she finally did start driving real
runs, she learned how to baby the most difficult
passengers, and her reputation got her all sorts
of requests. If there was an important party,
folks wanted the considerate and handsome
young driver who had never overturned a coach.
Ebeneezer just laughed out loud every time a
customer insisted on Charley, and no one else.

And her disguise? Charlotte carried on a mas-
querade same as an actor in a theater play. She
dressed carefully, wearing snug undershirts that
kept her figure boy-like. She wore loose-fitting,
pleated flannel shirts with a buckskin vest. She
favored baggy trousers, leather boots, a broad-
brimmed hat, and snug buckskin gloves. She
kept a snakeskin whip tucked into her belt.

And she didn't need to worry about her voice.
When she was out with the horses, she prac-
ticed speaking low. Maybe it was because she
was so good with those horses, or maybe it was
because the townspeople just didn't pay much
mind, but Ebeneezer's clean-shaven young driver

with the warm, raspy voice, just didn't arouse any suspicion. Charlotte was acting, dressing, and talking like a first-rate stage driver, so in folks' eyes, that's what she was.

Anyway, Charlotte was careful to protect her identity. She didn't bunk with the other stable-hands, still preferring to sleep in the loft, and for that, they teased her something fierce about loving horses more than people.

She was even cautious about the letters she wrote to Hayward. Instead of mailing them herself, she had other drivers mail them from towns all over the Atlantic Coast, and she had him write to her in care of Ebeneezer's stables. Now and then, Hayward would send word that he had ridden over near Concord and stopped at the orphanage to let Vern know her whereabouts. The words of encouragement that Vern sent back through Hayward always made her smile.

For six years, she managed to stay clear of Mr. Millshark. She was eighteen and fully grown, but she was still a young woman doing a man's work. If she was ever found out, her job could end in a moment's recognition.

And all of her dreams along with it.

6

WHAT CHEER STABLES, IN PROVIDENCE, Rhode Island, teemed with activity. There were plenty of passengers to carry as well as parcels of mail and strongboxes from the bank. Charlotte settled into a busy routine, caring for her horses and for her passengers. She was partial to the women and children, always respectful and giving them the best seats. The occasional grumbling men didn't complain too much, because the talk was they were riding with the best and safest driver on the whole Atlantic Coast.

Charlotte didn't have much time or cause for worry, until one morning when Ebeneezer handed her the manifest with the list of passengers. She froze at the name before her. It couldn't be the same Mr. Millshark, could it? Carefully Charlotte peeked from under her hat and studied the group of people standing near the ticket office. There was a group of women, two children, and one gentleman. The gentleman *was* Mr. Millshark, one and the same, dressed in a handsome gray suit. But something was peculiar about him. He had grown taller. Much taller. Then Charlotte noticed the fancy boots with high heels that made him look bigger than he actually was.

Suddenly, Charlotte felt twelve years old again. She knew she'd never have to go back to the orphanage. But her heart told her that there was more at stake. If he discovered her, he'd make sure people knew who she was and what she'd done. Once word got out, it wouldn't matter how old she was or how good a driver. Customers wouldn't ride with a woman.

When Ebeneezer saw Charlotte standing still, he said, "Charley, get to work!"

"I'll get the rear boot," said Charlotte, and she began loading the baggage in the leather storage behind the coach. She tied the overflow baggage on the roof of the carriage, double- and triple-checking the knots. She felt jittery, and her forehead broke out in beads of sweat. She took out her kerchief and dabbed at her brow.

Ebeneezer handed her the paperwork.

"You look like you seen a ghost," he said.

"I don't think I can drive today."

"What are you blabberin' about? The mail's gotta go through, same as them passengers."

Then Ebeneezer looked over at Mr. Millshark. He studied the man, and after a while, a feeling of recognition settled over him. Could it really be the same man from an orphanage who had come looking for a runaway girl some years ago?

Ebeneezer put his hand on Charlotte's shoulder. "Now listen, don't you pay them passengers no mind. You are what you are. And what you are, is a fine horseman. And the best coachman I ever saw. You remember that. Under the circumstances, there ain't nothing left for you to do but your job. So get to it."

Charlotte looked square at Ebeneezer.

Ebeneezer looked square back at Charlotte and said, "You're the coachman. You're in charge, so load 'em up."

Charlotte pulled her hat down lower over her face and tied her kerchief over her nose. She hoped Ebeneezer was right.

"All aboard!" she yelled.

Charlotte seated the women first and put them by the windows. Those were the best seats. Then she put in the children.

"Do you have a seat for me, good man?" asked Mr. Millshark.

"You can squeeze in on the middle bench with them children," said Charlotte.

"Could I persuade you with a few fine cigars to let me sit up-top since I'm just going to the next town?" he asked.

Charlotte hesitated. She didn't want to argue with Mr. Millshark any more than she had to. And any reputable stage driver would never turn down a handful of cigars.

"Certainly," she said stiffly, and climbed into the box seat, keeping her head turned away.

Pleased with himself, Mr. Millshark climbed up and sat next to Charlotte.

"Thank you," he said. "It'll be a pleasurable ride, for sure."

Two stock tenders brought the lead horses

out, positioned them in the traces, and handed the ribbons to Charlotte. Next came the swings, the middle horses in the lineup, and last came the wheelers, the horses closest to the wheels. The stock tenders released the leaders.

"Get along, my beauties!" yelled Charlotte.

With a flick of her wrist, the stagecoach lurched forward and Charlotte carefully maneuvered the stage out of town.

She allowed the horses to pick up speed. The coach began rollicking across the countryside, veering down the dusty road.

Thoroughbraces, three-inch straps of leather hooked to the axles, cradled the carriage like a baby in a hammock. The coach rocked back and forth. The passengers on the inside bounced around on padded seats but up top, where Charlotte and Mr. Millshark sat, there was nothing but a wooden bench.

Mr. Millshark, wedged into the corner of the box seat, held onto his hat with one hand, and clutched the narrow rail with the other.

Charlotte knew every twist in the road. She knew when she could speed up and when she should hold back. She remembered Ebeneezer's words: "You are a fine horseman and the best coachman I ever saw."

"Going a little fast, aren't you!" yelled Mr. Millshark.

"I know my horses by heart and I'm not one for bad drivin', so hold tight!" hollered Charlotte.

Nervously, he said, "You're the boss."

"Git aeoup!" she yelled, giving the horses more rein and enjoying this moment, this power over Millshark. She loved the thrill of being the master of her team. Charlotte looked at him. He seemed pitiful, hanging onto the rails for dear life. Why, she wasn't even going that fast!

She knew which roads might be flooded after a rain, which might be cluttered with branches after a storm, and which were muddy. A few days earlier, on this same road, she got stuck in a mud bog near Jenson's farm. Today, she would have to go around by another road to miss the bog, but suddenly, she felt some childish urge for revenge and had an idea. She gave the team a loud whistle and drove them directly toward the middle of the bog. The stagecoach mired in the doughy mud, but Charlotte wasn't worried.

The passengers weren't in any danger, and she'd still get them to their stops on time.

"Well, if that don't beat all!" said Charlotte.

"We're stuck," said Mr. Millshark.

"Let's get her out. You get some brush under her wheels so I can guide her to the other side," said Charlotte.

"I beg your pardon?" said Mr. Millshark.

"I'm the only one who can drive this team. Them women in the coach are only good for cookin' and sewin'. I need a strong man to help me. Or else we might be here till this mud dries up. I'd recommend takin' off those fancy boots and them fine stockings though."

Mr. Millshark reluctantly peeled them off and got down from the coach. He sank in the mud up to his ankles. He picked up his feet slowly, sinking farther into the mud with each step. He dragged some tree branches over and placed them under the wheels of the stagecoach.

Inside, the coach was cozy, paneled with basswood, and lit with oil lanterns with brass fittings. The small windows had leather shades that could be pulled down to protect the passengers from weather or dust.

"Pull down those window shades, ladies," Charlotte yelled. "Don't want you to get muddy!"

Trying not to chuckle, Charlotte stayed up in the box seat and worked the horses back and forth. Each time the wheels turned, Mr. Millshark got sprayed with mud. Finally, Charlotte maneuvered the stage out of the bog and waited farther up the road than she needed for Mr. Millshark to catch up.

"Good man," said Charley. "Thank you."

Mr. Millshark climbed up top, but didn't say a word. On the way to the next town, Charlotte drove as fast as was safe. When she glanced at Mr. Millshark, he looked as pale as milk. It was hours later when Charlotte stopped the stage.

"Well, here we are, the first stop," she said.

"My boots?" said Mr. Millshark.

Charlotte looked around.

"They were here, sure as I'm here," said Charlotte. "They must have dropped out on the way. That's a pity. Well, I suppose we could go back and take a look for them?"

"No!" said Millshark. "I mean, no need." He held out a coin and said, "If you see those boots again, I'd appreciate you retrieving them. They were specially ordered. Very expensive."

"Yes, sir," said Charlotte. She took the coin and hopped down from the seat. She pulled off the kerchief from her face and busied herself with the baggage.

Mr. Millshark was covered with a dried crust of mud and still complaining about his sore bottom and lost boots. He climbed down and came over to Charlotte.

Charlotte looked at him, nodded, and handed him his bags.

A glimmer of recognition crossed Mr. Millshark's face.

"You look familiar," he said.

"Oh, that's what lots of folks say," said Charlotte, and she hopped back up in the box seat and readied the horses before he could respond.

Mr. Millshark had a puzzled look on his face as he walked, barefooted, into the hotel.

And hidden in the leather storage were a new pair of boots for Ebeneezer.

7

TWO OF EBENEEZER'S STABLE BOYS,
James Birch and Frank Stevens, had left Rhode
Island some years ago for California. Now they
were back and as excited as two puppy dogs
about their adventures. They were full of stories about Argonauts, the gold diggers, and
Charlotte couldn't get enough of their tales.

The West was wild and untamed. Prospec-
tors flocking to pan for gold up and down the
lower Sierras were becoming millionaires
overnight. And Sacramento. Everyone was talking about Sacramento, California, the most important river port in the West. It was a
boom-town and for a businessman it was as

tempting as a candy store because if a man struck it rich, he had to have someplace to take his gold and someplace to spend his worth.

"People got to get from one place to another," said James. "So we started a small stage line, but now we're joinin' with other lines to start the California Stage Company. And we need good drivers. We need men in the Mother Lode, where all the gold is. Where they're mining. And we're planning to expand routes up and down the Pacific Coast so you'd have your pick. Won't you come, Charley?"

The money was good and there was plenty of work for men that would go. But what interested Charlotte most was the talk about land.

"If you're looking to own any, it's cheap and plentiful," said Frank.

Charlotte couldn't help but be excited.

James persisted. "We've secured boat passage from Atlanta to Panama. You would travel overland by mule through Panama, then secure a ship to San Francisco, and then take a riverboat to Sacramento. It's a month's journey. But when you get there, there's land as far as the eye can see, just waiting to be bought by you, Charley."

Their enthusiasm was catching.

"Well, boys, that land sounds mighty appealing," said Charlotte.

"C'mon, Charley. You're the best driver we know and we need you," said James.

Charlotte knew from the minute they started talking about the land that she would go. But she had to tell Ebeneezer. And that wouldn't be easy.

"It ain't a pony ride out there in California!" Ebeneezer practically shouted. "In some places there ain't roads, just worn-down trails made by pack mules that went afore you. The ground is filled with chuckholes and you'll be knee-deep in dust!"

"Yes, sir, but I need to go," said Charlotte.

"You don't know what you're in for. Most of the horses are just wild mustangs they brought in from the foothills that don't know how to work in the traces. You'll only make three miles an hour on a good day!"

He paced back and forth.

"I hear the coaches are so loaded with folks headed for the mining towns that they have to put passengers on the roof! You'll lose 'em off the top! And . . . and you got other things to consider. California ain't no place for a . . . for a . . . you know . . . for you!"

Ebeneezer had never, not once, said anything about Charlotte's secret. He never confronted her. He never asked her outright. But he knew. He rubbed his hands over his bald head.

Charlotte tried to explain.

"I aim to get me a ranch and I won't ever be able to afford it here in the East," she said. "Out West, there's land to be had. Cheap. I don't want to spend the rest of my life sleeping in a loft. I want to get me a place. My own place. A home."

He stopped pacing, crossed his arms and said, "What about Indians? You thought about that? And carryin' all that bullion? Why, a robber'll look at you and think you're a plum, ripe for pickin'."

Charlotte didn't answer him. She knew she was going. And so did he.

Ebeneezer sat down. He looked defeated.

"You're my best driver. I know I never said anything, but well, you remind me of somebody.

And it's just done my heart real good to see you outdo all them other drivers. All them other boys."

His voice drifted off.

"I had a child once. A girl. She died from the fever, same as my wife. But that little girl . . . she could ride like the wind. I ain't never seen anything like it . . . 'cept you."

He was quiet. Charlotte walked over and took his hand.

"I guess I put more stock in having you around than I should," he said. "I just hate to lose you to . . . to California."

Charlotte didn't want to lose Ebeneezer, either. He had been good to her. He had let her make her own way. He had protected her. Like a daughter.

"I just bet when I get my place you could come out and start a livery," said Charlotte. "You heard them boys talkin'. Sounds pretty exciting, don't it?"

His eyes perked up a little at the prospect.

"And I'll need you out there," she said. "I aim to get a bit of land. Why, I can't run a big place by myself."

"I guess I could think about it," said Ebeneezer. "Down the line. Guess I'm not too old to travel. Maybe someday."

They looked at each other. He half-smiled.

"Well, get going and pack your things. I told you a long time ago that workin' for me would be temporary. Don't you get harmed out there. And you need anything, you holler."

By now, Charlotte understood his blustery ways.

"Thank you," she said.

"What's your name anyway?" he grumbled.

She smiled and bent over and whispered it in his ear.

Charlotte stood on the top deck of the *Wilson G. Hunt*, a palace of a steamboat, while it chugged up the Sacramento River. She had been traveling for four weeks and a day and was anxious to reach Sacramento. She felt like she did that day on the stagecoach when she'd run away from the orphanage. Like she was on the verge of something exciting. Something new. Like she was closer to realizing her dream.

The delta sprawled in front of her. It was a

damp, green blanket met by gentle hills. Rivulets of water shimmered through the delta. Over the hills, there was land that stretched out forever. Speckled with a few trees and brush, it was just like Frank and James had said. Plenty of wide-open space, just waiting for her. As soon as she had enough money, she was going to buy her own property. Her own place. Then she would write Ebeneezer and Hayward and ask them to come, too.

When the boat docked in Sacramento, the port was a mass of confusion. Stagecoaches crowded in the street next to the docks, waiting for passengers. Armed marshals guarded strongboxes filled with gold dust waiting for the outbound boat to San Francisco. Porters cursed and swore and tossed parcels on the docks while dock handlers loaded the baggage onto the coaches. James said he'd meet the boat, but Charlotte didn't know how she'd ever find him.

Charlotte shoved her way through the crowd. Horses whinnied and pranced impatiently. Passengers disembarked around her and crowded into the street like an army of ants at a picnic.

Charlotte had never seen such confusion in her

life. She was jostled one way and another. She kept looking for James. There were so many people.

"Charley! Charley! Over here!"

Relieved, she spotted James trolling an extra horse.

"James! I don't know who I'm gladder to see, you or that horse."

"Climb on, Charley! Let's ride out of this mess."

Charlotte hadn't been on a horse in some weeks and it felt good to be riding again, and especially to be above the crowd. She moved the stallion slowly through the hustle of the docks and followed James toward the outskirts of town.

But as quickly as they got away from the docks, they rode into another street crowded with laughing, jeering men.

A woman stood on the steps of a saloon, passing out handbills to anyone who would take them.

"Wyoming Territory is already talking about giving women the right to vote," she called out. "If Wyoming can recognize a woman's rightful voice, then California should, too!"

"Then let the women move to Wyoming!" yelled one man, and the crowd cheered.

"With the men out in the mines, many women are running the farms and should be able to make decisions that affect their properties and families. Women have already organized in the East, have already held a Women's Rights Convention," she yelled back.

"Stick with cookin' and babies!" yelled another man, and the group let out a whoop of laughter. Most dropped the handbills on the ground and went inside. The others shook their heads and walked away. The womenfolk hurried about their business and many did not stop or look up, but Charlotte noticed a few picking up the handbills and tucking them into their pockets.

Charlotte got off the horse and headed toward the saloon steps.

"Charley, what're you up to?" hollered James.

She approached the woman.

"I'd like one of them handbills," said Charlotte.

The woman looked at Charlotte and handed over one of the papers.

"Are you prepared to laugh also?" she asked.

"No, ma'am," said Charlotte. "I would be interested to know who you would vote for in the upcoming political race."

The woman studied Charlotte's face for mockery.

Charlotte said again, "If you could vote, who would you vote for?"

While Charlotte listened, the woman explained her views on the candidates. She also told her about the convention in Seneca Falls, New York, and the women and *men* who gathered there in the name of women's rights.

When she had finished, the woman said, "You know, there are men who support our movement, too, young man."

"I agree with them men," said Charlotte, as she reached out and shook the woman's hand. Then Charlotte tipped her hat and said, "You are much braver than me."

She got back on the horse and left the surprised woman, standing on the saloon steps.

As she rode along, she read the handbill. She was familiar with politics. Stage drivers heard all the news from the passengers, and Charlotte had opinions of her own. She meant it when she told the woman that she was brave. It took

courage to stand up in front of all those laughing men. Charlotte wished she could have done something more for the lady.

"You sympathizin' with her?" asked James.

"It's interesting, that's all," said Charlotte.

"You're gonna find a lot of interesting things here. Things you ain't never seen in the East. But right now, let's get you settled."

A few miles out of Sacramento, James and Frank had converted a ramshackle building into a coach barn and stables. Outside, an impressive sign said CALIFORNIA STAGE COMPANY. Inside, Concord stagecoaches, the finest from the East, were lined up, waiting for the drivers' next runs. There was a bunkhouse for the hands, but since there wasn't a loft, Charlotte found a storeroom off the tack room that suited her fine.

"Everything's a bit makeshift, Charley," said James. "We aim to get things fixed up, but we got so much business we just ain't had the time. Everybody's in a hurry to get in and out of gold country. And time is money."

"How many drivers you got? And where are the horses?" asked Charlotte.

"We're startin' with ten stage whips at this stable, and already that ain't enough. But we're only takin' good drivers. And the horses, well, that's another thing we're makin' do with. I already bought a number of blooded stock horses from Australia and paid a small fortune for a particular strong stallion. I'm gonna make this a reputable line with quality service. But the horses haven't arrived yet. We rounded up some mustangs. They'll need to be shoed first thing in the mornin'. You ready to meet some western horses?"

"Tame or otherwise?" asked Charlotte.

James laughed. "Welcome to California, Charley! Here, everything's wild!"

8

TWO STOCK TENDERS HELD A NERVOUS
horse by ropes tied to the bridle's cheek straps.
Ebeneezer had been right. Many of the horses
were feral and had never been broken, and that
made them even harder to shod. Charlotte got
into position and pulled up the back hoof. The
horse reared.

The last thing Charlotte remembered was the
hoof coming toward her face.

And the pain.

She woke up in the doctor's office and tried to
sit up but reeled from the headache. Her stomach churned. She retched.

Charlotte reached up and felt her left eye. It

was swollen shut and scraped and bloody. She tried to open it, but the lid would only lift part way.

"What happened?" Charlotte asked. She nervously checked to see that she was fully dressed.

"It's best to lie still," said the doctor. "You were kicked in the face by a wild horse. Mr. Birch brought you in and waited for some time. I assured him I'd take good care of you, but that I needed to keep you here overnight. I'm afraid you might lose the sight in that eye. What's a girl trying to shoe a horse for?"

"What?" Charlotte said.

"You're dressed like a young man and those hands are calloused like a ranch hand. But I'm a doctor and I know a girl when I see one."

He stared at Charlotte.

"I-I need my job," said Charlotte. "And I couldn't work if anybody knew . . . if Mr. Birch knew . . ."

"You don't need to give me a long drawn-out explanation. You're not the first woman pretending to be a man that I've ever treated. I'm not going to tell anyone, including Mr. Birch.

Now don't move a minute. I'm going to put on this ointment."

Charlotte flinched as the doctor dabbed on a foul-smelling medicine.

"I've got one lady out past town whose husband's been gone to the gold mines for two years and nobody thinks he's gone. She's been pretending to be him all this time. Saved her from many a problem. Had another patient some years ago whose husband was killed by bandits. She dressed in his clothes for several years to protect herself and her children in the wilderness. Held off a few raids and everyone thought it was him. When her sons got old enough, she changed back and told everyone the true story. Don't you worry about me."

"What about my eye?" asked Charlotte.

"When the swelling and bruising goes down, we'll know more, but it'll be cockeyed, at least. And like I said, it might be blind."

"How soon till I can drive again?" asked Charlotte.

"You won't be driving any time soon," said the doctor. "And I don't know anyone who would hire a driver with only one good eye."

Charlotte felt sick again. She didn't know if it was from the pain or from her bad luck. She hadn't even driven a single stage run in California and now she couldn't see out of one eye. How would she work? How would she get enough money to buy property? She wished Ebeneezer was here. Or Hayward. But they were three thousand miles away.

She lay back down on the doctor's table and the room swirled around her. She retched again.

The next day, Charlotte waited on the bench in front of the doctor's office for James to come and get her. She couldn't see a thing out of her left eye. She looked at the black eye patch she held in her hand, but the doctor said it couldn't be worn until her eye healed. People walking by were alarmed when they saw her. Some stared and then turned away, except for the children, who just plain stared. Others stopped and asked questions like it was their business. Charlotte slumped over and kept her head down.

She had spent years trying to blend in and not be noticed and now everyone walking by examined her face. She was self-conscious and embarrassed. One little child started crying when he saw her. She felt like a monster.

Finally, James pulled up in a wagon.

"Charley, you look like you wrestled a bull and the bull won," he said. "C'mon now, let's get you back to the stable."

Riding back, Charlotte had only one thing on her mind. "James, how soon till I can drive?"

"Frank and I already discussed it. You can't drive with only one good eye. We can't take a chance. Not with business so good and our names at stake. But you can stock tender for us for as long as you like. That's the best we can do."

After Charlotte got back to the stables, she shut the door of the small storeroom and lay down on the bunk. Silent tears stung the cuts and scrapes on her hurt eye and blurred the other. How am I going to get where I'm going if I can't see? she thought. The crying made her bad eye swell even more. But just like that day at the orphanage when Hayward left, once she started, she couldn't stop until every tear was given away.

With the eye patch, Charlotte looked a little

like a pirate and folks around the livery started calling her One-eyed Charley. She didn't mind because people accepted the eye patch much easier than they did a crooked, deformed eye. What she did mind was not being able to drive. As much as she tried to be grateful for her job, her heart wasn't in it. She ached to get out and ride the countryside. She had learned to love the freedom of driving as much as she loved her animals. The feeling of being in charge. Of folks trusting that she knew the way. And of knowing her team. When she drove, her horses seemed almost to know what would be expected of them without a word being spoken. Sometimes, it seemed like magic.

After a month, Charlotte was itching to sit in the box seat. And since stock tenders didn't make nearly as much as stage drivers, she missed the money, too.

One moonlit night, Charlotte walked around the back of the stables and caught her reflection in a barrel of water. She looked hard at herself. She lifted the eye patch. Her left eye was crooked and twisted. Her face had weathered. Her hair was straight and too long. Like most ranch hands, she had it pulled back and tied in a tail. It was a knotted mess from being under a hat. She smoothed her cheeks with her hands, hardly recognizing herself.

She remembered another night long ago when she had looked at herself in a pool of water. What had she wanted back then? She had wanted to be out of the kitchen and riding horses. She had wanted to find Hayward again someday and to have a ranch of her own. She'd been stubborn enough to think that somehow she could do it all. Now her dreams were slipping away, and it frightened her clear to the bone. Riding coaches was the reason she'd come to California. And it was the way she was going to make it here.

She took out her kerchief and dipped the corner in the water and wiped her face. What had Vern told her? That she had to do what her heart tells her.

"The only way to get my ranch is to keep riding and driving horses," she whispered to herself. "And that's what I aim to do."

The next afternoon, while Frank and James went into town for their daily bank run, she

took a six-horse team out on her own. She had to see if she could still drive.

The straight parts weren't bad. The horses knew the road. Charlotte held the reins and gave the tugs. But veering to the left was a problem because she couldn't see much to the left. She ran the coach off the road and up an embankment. It was a struggle to get the horses out of the soft dirt and back on the road.

"Now I'll know what *not* to do next time," she said to the horses.

The next day, she overturned the coach completely but was able to jump free. What was she doing wrong? She knew how to drive a team. She didn't need training with the horses or the ribbons. She knew those things by heart. It was her eye she didn't know. She needed to train her one good eye. She needed to learn how to use it all over again.

She started taking a smaller team out every day. First a two-horse team. Then a four. Finally, with six-in-the-hand. Charlotte had been proving herself her whole life and she wasn't about to stop now. She didn't even care if Frank and James caught on to what she was doing. They might as well see me trying, she thought.

She learned the different sounds the horses' hooves made on different types of roads. If the road was hard, the hooves made a hollow, clopping sound. If the road was soft, the hooves made a dull, thudding sound. She relied on her one good eye to take over for the other. She trusted her senses. And the sixth sense she had for handling horses.

Charlotte drove back and forth over her route and memorized every rock and tree. She set a goal for herself. If she made ten clean, round-trip runs, she'd know she was as good as the next driver. After that, she'd just have Frank and James to convince.

After the tenth clean run, Charlotte went to James. "I want to drive the stage run over the river."

"Now, Charley, we've been over all that. Me and Frank think . . ."

"You ride with me, and if you don't think I'm fit, then I won't bother you again," said Charlotte.

"What will the passengers say about your eye patch?" said James.

"Just tell them it's to frighten off bandits. They won't know any different."

"I don't know . . ."

Charlotte defended herself. "You know my reputation. I traveled all this way. Riding coaches is the whole reason I came to California. And I came because you asked me to come. You know I been practicin'. Go by my past drivin'. That's all I'm askin', and I wouldn't be askin' if I didn't know I could drive."

Reluctantly, James said, "The first sign that you can't handle the situation, I take the reins."

"I'll tell you if I need help. Don't go steppin' in unless I ask."

"Fair enough," said James.

"Tomorrow?"

"Tomorrow, if the weather holds."

"I ain't going to be a fair-weather driver," said Charlotte. "I want to drive, same as usual, like all the other drivers."

"Well, I guess you deserve that much. Tomorrow, rain or shine."

It was one of those storms where the rain came down in washtubs, but the stage was scheduled to go. The coach was chock-full of passengers, baggage, and mail pouches that had to get through. Charlotte was soaked clear through by the time the baggage was secured. James rode shotgun next to her.

The wind wouldn't let up, and the rain came flying in every which direction. James seemed nervous.

"Charley, I can't even see the road!" he yelled.

"Then it's a good thing I'm drivin', 'cause I can smell it, and I can hear it!" yelled Charlotte.

James sat back as the coach headed into the storm. The mud was so thick it reached the hubs, but Charlotte still found the road.

When they reached the river, it had swelled almost to the bridge supports. Charlotte stopped the stage on the north bank.

"Stay inside," she told the passengers. "I'll be checkin' the bridge."

Charlotte took off her gloves and carefully walked across the swaying timbers to see if the bridge was worthy. She stomped a few times and listened to the moans of the wood. She felt the swollen planks and pulled on the guard ropes until she was satisfied.

She walked back to the stage and told the passengers to get out.

"Ain't no reason to risk your lives," said Charlotte. "James, I'm going to walk you and these fine people over to the other side to wait for me there."

But a portly gentleman refused to budge.

"I'll take my chances inside the coach," he said.

"Not on my coach," said Charlotte.

"I'm familiar with adventure, young man," he argued.

"The bridge can't take any extra weight, and I'm not about to lose my first passenger to that river. Now, step out or I'll help you step out."

Still grumbling, the man reluctantly climbed down.

In the blinding rain, Charlotte escorted the group, a few at a time, across the bridge. When they were safely settled on the other side, she walked back for the stage.

She got back in the box. Thunder growled nearby. She knew what was coming next. She held tight to the ribbons and waited for the lightning. It hit within a mile but she kept the horses reined. Trusting her instincts, she inched the horses and the stage across the bridge. The timbers groaned as the iron-capped wheels clacked across the wooden planks. Ahead, the passengers huddled together and watched anxiously from the other side. The river raced a few feet beneath the wheels.

The bridge rocked and the horses reared and whinnied. The coach was smack in the middle of the bridge.

Charlotte kept her sights on the far bank.

She heard the splintering and cracking of weathered wood that meant the bridge was coming apart.

Tree limbs swayed in the wind and the sounds of the storm brought back a memory from somewhere deep in Charlotte's mind. A jumble of frantic images and words. Being held in someone's lap. And voices. "Stop! Hold on!" Her parents' voices. And a face. Yes, her mother's face close to hers. "Keep them straight! Keep them straight!" That's what she had to do.

She stood up in the box. "Keep them straight on the bridge, Charlotte." Dashing the water from her good eye and gathering the reins in a firm grip, she cracked her whip and yelled, "Away!"

She was thrown back into the box. The horses jibbed, side to side, but she held tight to the ribbons. They flew across like scared jackrabbits. The back wheels barely turned on solid ground when the bridge collapsed and dropped into the churning river.

"Whoa, my beauties! Whoa!" yelled Charlotte.

The passengers hurried back to the stage, clamoring about the excitement, while Charlotte settled the team.

"We could've all fallen in," one woman gasped.

"My heart's a-pounding," a man exclaimed as others joined him.

"We would've drowned."

"He saved my life!" said the gentleman who had almost refused to leave the coach.

And by the way they were talking and James was nodding his head, Charlotte knew there wouldn't be a question about her driving a stage again.

9

THE PASSENGERS' TONGUES WERE wagging long after the coach arrived at its destination. News of how the one-eyed stage driver saved the lives of those people spread like warm honey. For years after that, Charlotte caused all sorts of commotion every time she drove into town. Folks started tossing three-dollar gold pieces in the road to see if she could hit them with the wheels of the stagecoach. Seems that, if a one-eyed driver could run over your coin, you'd have good luck.

Grown men would stand on the side of the road and wait for the stage to come through. Children running behind the stage collected the coins and delivered them, like offerings to a hero. And folks just gathered around to hear what One-eyed Charley had to say, though as usual, that wasn't much.

"Here, Charley, you hit this one," one little girl said, giggling.

"My pockets are already jangling," Charlotte said.

"Papa says you're not scared of nothing," said another.

"That's not true. I'm as scared as you are," said Charlotte. "I just do what I have to do."

"What ya gonna buy with all that money?" asked a small boy.

Charlotte said, "I'm going to buy somethin' I've wanted since I was knee-high."

"A new horse?" said the boy.

"Nope," said Charlotte.

"A new gun?"

"Nah, I got one already and don't use it 'cept to scare off bandits," said Charlotte. "It's somethin' much better than both of them things."

Charlotte was driving a new route from San Juan Bautista to Santa Cruz. She had moved from Sacramento and was sleeping in a barn loft again, but this time at a way station, where the stage drivers changed horses. Frank and James had promised her that it was a beautiful run. They were right. It was the kind of country that Charlotte loved. Toward the East, mountains, and in the West, rolling hills that sometimes met the ocean. It was greener than Sacramento, and Charlotte even liked the fog that made the mornings last longer. But the way station was another story.

Stage drivers changed horses every twelve miles and most of the way stations were pitiful, including this one. It was a dirty, run-down stable for fifteen or so horses. If the passengers had to spend the night, they slept in a hut on a dirt floor. The food was mostly rancid bacon, mustard greens, corn doggers, and sandy coffee. Now that she had the money, Charlotte couldn't wait to move. Couldn't wait to buy her own place.

One afternoon, while riding a horse toward Watsonville to mail a letter to Hayward, she saw a FOR SALE sign in a pasture. She turned her horse down the road and at the end, there was a cabin with a few corrals. A sturdy, gray-haired woman came out of a rustic chicken coop with a basket of eggs on her arm. As she walked, she held herself tall.

"You here about the property?"

"Yes, ma'am," said Charlotte.

"The owners don't live here anymore. I'm Margaret. I got the small house farther down the main road. I feed the chickens and collect the eggs."

"You know anything about the land?" asked Charlotte.

"Well, best I know it's twenty-five acres. There's an apple orchard that needs tendin' real bad. Forty layin' hens. Front pasture runs all the way to the main road to town."

Charlotte looked out toward the main road. That acreage would make a perfect way station. She knew that if she could get Ebeneezer out here, he'd do a finer job than anyone managing it.

Charlotte turned her attention back to the woman. "Any other neighbors?"

"I'm the closest," said Margaret. "But it don't look like for long. I was widowed last year and my husband still owed money on the mortgage. I been tryin' to keep up the payments. I sell the eggs in town to get by, but the bank's threatenin' to foreclose.

"Where're you movin'?" asked Charlotte.

"Well, now that's a quand'ry," she said, looking out over the land. "Lived here most of my days but don't have family. Don't want to leave, but I can't pay, and the bank . . . well, they need their money." For an instant, her face clouded over and her warm brown eyes reflected sadness.

"If you're looking for another bit of land, I guess the bank would sell you mine in a hurry," said Margaret. "Well, I'll be on my way. Good luck, young man," and she turned and walked down the road.

Charlotte surveyed the property. She had known the moment she came down the lane that it was the land she'd been looking for. She'd saved a substantial amount of money. She could afford it. As she rode to the bank to inquire though, instead of thinking about the twenty-five acres and the home she could finally own, she couldn't get her mind off Margaret and the home she stood to lose.

A few days later, Charlotte offered six hundred dollars in gold coin for the property. The bank president handed Charlotte a pen. She signed the papers.

"You just bought a fair portion of what is called Rancho Corralitos," said the president.

"Thank you," said Charlotte. "Tell me about that land to the west, the small parcel where the widow lives."

"The wife can't pay so we're foreclosing. She hasn't got a cent. Hate to do it, but women usually can't pay and after all, business is business."

Charlotte nodded.

The bank president grabbed Charlotte's hand and pumped it up and down. "Congratulations. It's been a pleasure, Mr. Parkhurst."

It all happened so fast that afterward, as Charlotte stood on the bank steps, smiling, she wondered if it had been a dream.

She couldn't resist riding back out to see the place again. It was late afternoon as she turned down the road. Her road. The sky clouded and the early evening mist settled in the air. When she reached the hillock, she stopped and looked out over her land.

The west wind blew a breeze off the Pacific. The pasture grass swayed in one continuous, rolling wave. Pinkish dots showed on the orchard trees as the apples ripened. Charlotte's heart filled at the sight of it. I did it, she thought. I did it. She saw herself picking the apples and raising horses, and she pictured Hayward right alongside her, training the horses to be ridden, just like they had imagined all those years ago at the orphanage. But as proud as she was that she had done what she set out to do, there was a part of her that felt like something was missing. After all, this had been Hay's dream, too.

That night she would write to Ebeneezer and tell him if he had any sense, he should come. She needed him to start the way station. Besides, she missed him. Then she would write to Hayward and tell him the news. But it had been so many months since she'd heard from him. Had something happened to him? Was his heart settled in a new place and he didn't want to tell her?

Mail being what it was, it could take a month

for a letter to travel east and a month to get an answer. But Charlotte went to the post office every few days anyway. When she heard from Ebeneezer, Charlotte grinned ear to ear and let out a loud whoop. He was coming for a visit in the spring and if he liked it, he'd stay. She couldn't wait to see him again. Maybe by then she'd have some horses.

Charlotte moved into her house. And since business was business, she had gone back to that bank president and purchased Margaret's small parcel of land to the west. Then, she and Margaret had struck an agreement: Margaret tended the chickens and eggs and did some cooking, and that was enough rent for Charlotte.

Another four months passed. The chickens were well cared for and there were plenty of fresh eggs to sell. Margaret made applesauce, apple butter, and preserves. Charlotte hoped Ebeneezer liked apples, because he'd be eating them every which way.

Charlotte rode home one evening, tired and dusty. She was familiar with every shadow of her property but, in the waning light, she could tell that something was wrong. She stared hard in the dim light with her good eye to figure out what it was. In the front pasture there was something different. Something wooden. A box? Who would have left a wood box in her front pasture?

After she first moved in, she had found a burlap sack tossed down her road. It was a litter of kittens that someone had abandoned. She took them in and nursed them all, and now they ran all over her orchard. Had someone tried to leave another poor animal on her property? This time in a wooden box?

As she rode closer, she realized that it wasn't a wooden box at all, but a sign. Someone had pounded a wooden sign in her front pasture and had painted some words on the front. Puzzled, she walked her horse through the tall pasture grass so she could get a good look.

Her heart leaped at the sight. She turned the horse and galloped toward the cabin.

Painted on the sign were the words PRIVATE PROPERTY.

Sitting on her front porch, playing with an armful of kittens, was a lanky, broad-shouldered,

red-haired man with the biggest ears Charlotte
had ever seen.

"Hayward!"

She tied her horse and bounded up the porch.
She hugged him long and hard.

"Hay, you're taller than me and twice as
strong. I don't think I can stand it!" said
Charlotte.

"It's about time I could be better than you at
something," he said, laughing.

They studied each other. Hay had never seen
Charlotte's eye patch before and she was suddenly embarrassed.

"I'm . . . I'm plumb blind in that eye," she
said.

"You don't look much different," said Hay.
"But you would scare William to death."

They both laughed. Memories of the orphanage flooded over Charlotte. When Hay reached
for a runaway kitten, Charlotte noticed the thin
leather tied around his wrist.

"You still got the leather bracelet?" she said
and held out her arm next to his to compare.
Both leather bands were soft and rolled from
years of wear.

"Remember that day, Charlotte?"

"As well as you," she said. They hugged again. So many years had passed between them. They were older, but everything about him seemed familiar.

"I . . . I missed you, Charlotte."

"Me, too, Hay."

Charlotte had been so hungry to see him that all she could do was stare. She started to reach up and ruffle his hair, but when she hesitated, an awkward silence came over them.

He finally said, "Well, I made it to California."

And when she remembered her manners, she said, "Sit down and tell me what you've been doing."

"Well, after my folks moved to Missouri, I rode for Pony Express, but that didn't last long. About a year and a half. The transcontinental telegraph and the railroad took its place right quick. After that, I needed work so I moved cattle for a while and I been stock tendering some." He grinned. "Been saving my money for California."

Charlotte smiled. It was the same old Hay,

chattering away, as eager as ever to tell her everything. She relaxed. Nothing had changed.

"Now my folks want to move west so when I got the chance to ride out with a wagon train, I knew I had to come, to learn the roads. And to see you. That's where I've been all these months. On the wagon train. I saved every one of your letters. I can't believe it's you, Charlotte."

"I know it's hard to believe, but I'm the same old Charlotte. Fightin' and scrappin' my way."

"You still driving?" he asked.

"Some. I aim to make my property the way station. Change the teams when they come through. I'll take care of the horses and buy a few of my own with the money I bring in. Ebeneezer's coming for a visit, and I'm going to do my best to get him to stay. For all my travel-ing around, I didn't ever think I'd want to stay put, but for some reason, I'm as contented as my new mare."

"You got a new mare? Will she foal in the spring?" he asked.

"Yep," she said.

He nodded his head and grinned. "I guess

we're as far away from the orphanage as we'll ever get."

"What do you hear about the orphanage?"

"Well, I saw some of the boys now and then. Last I heard, Millshark's still there but Mrs. Boyle's gone. I heard William got adopted the year after me by an elderly couple who needed someone to work their farm. I guess the man loved his animals and William beat his prize mare so they sent him back. First boy in years that got unadopted. Don't that figure. You heard about Vern? That he passed on?"

"No," said Charlotte quietly. "I didn't know, but for some reason, I suspected. He was getting on in years when we were there. I won't ever be forgetting him for what all he done for me."

Charlotte got teary-eyed and didn't even try to hide it. She pulled out her kerchief and wiped her eyes.

Hayward looked around the cabin. "You done good, Charlotte. You done real good."

10

HAYWARD STAYED FOR A MONTH OF
Sundays, and Charlotte couldn't bear thinking
about him leaving again.

The morning he left she said, "Hay, you can
stock tender for me as long as you like."

"Charlotte, I'm beginning to think you like
having me around," he teased. "I never thought
I'd see the day. But first, I got work to finish in
Missouri. Then I got to help my folks move out
here."

He hesitated, then said, "Charlotte, come
with me."

Charlotte looked out the window as if she
hadn't heard him.

"It'll take me over a year, Charlotte. You could get someone to watch the place. And then Ebeneezer could take over till we got back. Won't you come?"

She turned and looked at him. "I can't, Hay. I don't want to leave. I worked my whole life for this. I belong *here*. I want to build up my horse stock, and I got apples to pick, and things I got to do. Besides, there's something I been thinking on for some time that I feel real strongly about."

She knew she could tell Hay anything but she wasn't sure how he'd react to this. "I registered to vote in Santa Cruz County. The election's in a few weeks, and I don't want to miss it."

Hayward stared at her and shook his head. "Charlotte, you'll be going against the law."

"Hay, I know more about who to vote for than most. Women are citizens of this country just like you. They work hard and make decisions sound as a man's."

"There's a lot of folks who don't agree."

"There's a lot of *men* who don't agree," said Charlotte.

Hayward grinned at her.

"I ain't one of them," he said. "I just don't

understand what you'll be provin' if no one *knows* you're a woman."

"I guess I'm proving that here I am, a member of this county that most folks respect. Most of them ask *me* who *I'm* voting for! And the only reason I can walk in and vote is because they *think* I'm a man. Sooner or later, they'll all know I was a woman and my point will be made."

"So, someday you're gonna let people know you're a lady?" he asked.

"Maybe. But whether I let them know or not, I'll be wearin' these same clothes and tendin' my horses and runnin' this ranch, same as always."

He considered what she said and shook his head. "You know your mind, Charlotte, and that's fine by me. You know how I feel about you."

"I know."

He gave her a big hug and acted like he was never going to let go. Then he got on his horse and rode down the lane, past the corral. Charlotte stood on the porch and watched him ride away. He stopped halfway down the road and waved his hat.

Charlotte waved back.

He put his hat back on and cupped his hands around his mouth.

"I'll be back," he hollered.

"I know," Charlotte whispered to herself.

It was sprinkling when Charlotte rode into town that November afternoon, but a little rain couldn't stop her. She hoped it wouldn't stop other folks from getting out and doing what they had to do, either. Luckily, by the time she got to town, the sun had come out. She hitched the mustang and walked down the street and nodded to the people walking by. A big sign in the window of the hotel said POLLS. Some of the ladies in town went about their errands and didn't seem to give a second thought to the long line of men in front of the hotel. Others gathered out front, in twos and threes, waiting for their menfolk, and acted like there was nothing special going on inside. Charlotte wondered if they really didn't care. Or if they were going about playing their roles like she was playing hers.

One man came up and clapped her on the back.

"Glad to see ya, Charley," he said.

Another man said, "Pretty excitin' day, ain't it, Charley?"

Charlotte didn't say much. She shook hands all around and got in line with the men. She listened to them banter and joke around her.

"Heard Wyoming's gonna give women the right to vote. I thought I'd heard everything."

"What's this country comin' to?"

"What do you think, Charley?"

Charlotte said, "I don't think it hurts nothin'. Guess they know their minds as well as us."

"Don't hurt nothin'! Them women fightin' for this is just plain crazy, stirrin' up trouble all over. They'll be the ruination of this country. I told my wife that she wouldn't ever be votin' as long as she's married to me, no matter what the law says. What does she know about politics?"

Several other men added their opinions.

The line inched up the hotel steps.

A little boy ran up, found his father in line, and tugged on his hand.

"Papa, Papa! The Tayor boy said Sarah and I can't play ball 'cause I'm little and she's a girl. And she's fightin' him in the street and he's twice as big as her. Hurry, Papa!"

The father shook his head. "We told her and told her about fightin'. When's that girl gonna learn?"

The men chuckled, and the father and the little boy left.

The line moved closer to the desk.

Charlotte got to the front and signed the book.

The registrar handed her the ballot. She studied the names. Horatio Seymour or Ulysses S. Grant, the conservative Democrat or the much talked-about Republican. She had listened to the talk and heard people's debates. She had heard good things and bad things about both men but she knew her own mind and what she thought was right.

"You know who you're votin' for, Charley?" asked the man next to her.

"Yes, I do," said Charlotte.

"Old Jake couldn't make it today because he's ailin'. Felt real bad about not comin', but I told him one vote won't make no difference."

Charlotte nodded to the man. Would her one vote make a difference? Why was she doing this? Someday when people found out, would they just think that she had been crazy, too? Or would they wonder that she had a good reason?

Yes, she told herself. She had a good reason.

This was something she could do for that woman who stood up in front of all those laughing men and passed out handbills on the saloon steps. Something for those women out front who were pretending they didn't mind that they couldn't vote. For Vern, who hadn't been allowed to speak up and should have been able to. And for that little girl outside who was already standing up for herself.

She smiled. And for me, she thought. Because I'm as qualified as the next man.

She marked her choice for president of the United States.

She turned in her ballot, then faced the crowd of men still waiting in line. She tipped her hat.

"Gentlemen," she said, "may the best man win."

Then she walked out of the hotel, got on her horse, and rode home.

In the End

EBENEEZER ARRIVED IN THE SPRING, just before the foal. He surveyed the property and grumbled about all the things that should be done. The pasture fence needed mending and the chickens needed a new coop. Margaret needed help selling the eggs in town. Charlotte was tickled because she figured all his belly-aching meant he'd come to stay.

And the foal? It came in the middle of the night. In the middle of a thunderstorm. It gave Charlotte fits and worries because it was breach, trying to come out the wrong way. She coaxed as best she knew, but when she was afraid they'd both be lost, she woke up Ebeneezer.

The two sat up all night soothing the mother horse who was as frightened by the thunder as she was by the birthing. While Ebeneezer tried to deliver the foal, Charlotte paced like an expectant father. Her mind was on the night she sat up with Freedom. And she was remembering Vern. If he were here, he'd be telling her to settle down. That Ebeneezer knew what he was doing. Vern had been right about so many things.

But Charlotte needn't have worried. By the time the rooster crowed, a wet, folded-up bundle of legs was delivered. A filly.

The baby horse barely stood on her wobbly legs when Ebeneezer said, "There's another one coming! Twins!"

And in a few frantic minutes, a colt stood next to his sister.

"What're you gonna name them?" asked Ebeneezer. "You should call them Worry and Trouble for the night they gave us." And then he laughed.

But Charlotte got quiet and serious-like. "Naming something's important," she said. "And a name should stand for something. A horse's name should be fitting for a fine animal."

She watched the foals and didn't say anything. The mare licked the colt and the filly started nursing. And after she'd considered them for some time, Charlotte crossed her arms and nodded her head with a knowing smile. It had come to her.

"Well, you gonna keep it to yourself?" said Ebeneezer.

Charlotte was right proud to explain her

reasoning behind it all. And when she was finished, Ebeneezer had to agree. They were fine names. Important names that stood for something and were fitting for fine animals.

She named the colt, Vern's Thunder.

And she named the filly, Freedom.

From the Author

THIS FICTIONAL NOVEL IS BASED ON THE true story of Charlotte Darkey Parkhurst, also known as One-eyed Charley, Cockeyed Charley, and Six-horse Charley. Following is a synopsis of her life, derived from research.

She was born in some part of New Hampshire in 1812 and lived in an orphanage or poorhouse. She went to Worcester, Massachusetts, where she worked as a stable boy in Ebeneezer Balch's stables and remained there until Mr. Balch moved his business to Providence, Rhode Island. There she continued to work for him at What Cheer Stables, at that time located in the rear of the Franklin House Inn. Considered an expert stage driver, she worked for Mr. Balch for a number of years. For a brief period she left for Atlanta and then returned to Providence and worked in several other stables.

About 1849, James E. Birch and Frank Stevens went to California, and a few years later, consolidated several small stage lines into the California Stage Company. They recruited Charley to work for them. Shortly after arriving in California, Charlotte lost the use of one eye from a horse kick to the face.

Still posing as a male, by the 1860s, she was a noted

"whip" or "jehu" (a Biblical term referring to a charioteer) of the time. Charlotte retired from driving at a ranch near Watsonville, California.

Her name (Charles Darkey Parkhurst) is listed in the *Santa Cruz Sentinel* on October 17, 1868, under the official poll list, "Containing the names and Enrollment for all persons resident in the various Precincts in the County of Santa Cruz, State of California, registered up to October 4th, 1868, and entitled to vote at the Presidential Election."

Some historians think that Charlotte first voted on November 3, 1868, at Tom Mann's Hotel in downtown Soquel, California, where the Soquel Fire Station now stands.

After Charley's death, it was discovered that she was a woman. Deeds and records confirm that Charlotte, disguised as Charles Parkhurst, owned property in Watsonville. Charlotte's cabin was near the Seven Mile House, a former stagecoach stop and hotel. This way station for travelers on the Santa Cruz to Watsonville stage line was located on a road that was later named Freedom Boulevard. Charlotte also registered to vote in Santa Cruz County, fifty-two years before any woman would be allowed to vote in federal elections in the United States.

In 1955, the Pajaro Valley Historical Association marked her grave with a monument that reads:

CHARLEY DARKEY PARKHURST

1812-1879

NOTED WHIP OF THE GOLD RUSH DAYS

DROVE STAGE OVER MT. MADONNA IN

EARLY DAYS OF VALLEY. LAST RUN,

SAN JUAN TO SANTA CRUZ. DEATH IN

CABIN NEAR THE 7 MILE HOUSE

REVEALED "ONE EYED CHARLIE,"

A WOMAN, THE FIRST TO VOTE

IN THE U.S. NOV. 3, 1868

I have tried to keep the story line close to her real life but for the purposes of the novel, I sometimes had to take creative license. For instance, in actuality, Charlotte Parkhurst was born in 1812 and would have been 55 years old when she voted. I moved the time frame of the story to the mid-1800s, and spanned fewer years of her life, in consideration for young readers.

We will never really know Charlotte's motives for choosing to live her life the way she did. Possibly, she did what she had to do to survive during a time when there were very few opportunities for young women. I suspect that she stumbled upon the chance to become a stage driver, that she was good at it, and that it gave her personal freedoms that she would have never experienced as a girl. That freedom would have been very hard for anyone to give up once they had experienced it.

In the words of her obituary, "Who shall longer say that a woman can not labor and vote like a man?"

They had the **COURAGE** to believe in themselves.

Naomi's life with Gram is peaceful...until her mother reappears after seven years, stirring up questions and challenging Naomi to discover who she really is.

In Mexico, Esperanza lived like a princess. But after a sudden tragedy, she and her mother must start a new life in a California work camp.

A girl. A ghost horse.
An unforgettable journey

Paint the Wind

In grandmother's house, Maya feels like a prisoner. She is forbidden from playing or having friends, and even her memories of her mother have been erased. A world away, in a rugged landscape that Maya's mother once loved, a wild tobiano Paint horse runs free, belonging only to the stars—and she holds the key to Maya's memories.

BY PAM MUÑOZ RYAN
AUTHOR OF *ESPERANZA RISING*

■SCHOLASTIC
www.scholastic.com

WI